C000271607

Rain on the River

Also by Jim Dodge

Fup
Not Fade Away
Stone Junction

Jim Dodge

Rain ON THE River

Selected Poems and Short Prose

Grove Press
New York

Copyright © 2002 by Jim Dodge

All rights reserved. No part of this book may be reproduced
in any form or by any electronic or mechanical means,
including information storage and retrieval systems, without
permission in writing from the publisher, except by a
reviewer, who may quote brief passages in a review. Any
members of educational institutions wishing to photocopy
part or all of the work for classroom use, or publishers who
would like to obtain permission to include the work in an
anthology, should send their inquiries to Grove/Atlantic,
Inc., 841 Broadway, New York, NY 10003.

Published simultaneously in Canada
Printed in the United States of America

FIRST EDITION

Library of Congress Cataloging-in-Publication Data

Dodge, Jim.
    Rain on the River: selected poems and short prose/
    Jim Dodge, p. cm.
    ISBN 0-8021-3896-9
    1. Northwest, Pacific–Literary collections.   I. Title.

PS3554.O335 R35 2002   2001058483
813'.54–cc21

Grove Press
841 Broadway
New York, NY 10003

02 03 04 05   10 9 8 7 6 5 4 3 2 1

for

Victoria Stockley Dodge

covivant for over thirty years, the last seven as wife;
nerve of my soul, love of my life

Contents

Notes and Acknowledgments XI

Selected Poems and Short Prose

Learning to Talk 3
The Cookie Jar 4
Things Thought Through 7
On Balance 8
Decomposition 9
Psycho Ecology 10
Life of the Spirit 11
Aweigh 12
Tao-to-Tao 16
To Be 17
Practice, Practice, Practice 19
Wisdom and Happiness 20
Red Sails 22
Squall & Commotion 23
Slow Learner 24
Bathing Joe 25
Mahogany China 30
The First Cut Is the Deepest 31
Waiting for Houdini to Come Up 32
The Countessa 33
Venison Stew 35
Winter Song 37
On Humor: On Mating Donkeys and Onions 38
Watering the Garden on the Hottest Day
   of the Summer 39
Palms to the Moon 40
A Firmer Grasp of the Obvious 41
The Work of Art 42
Steelhead Fishing, Smith River, January 43

The Third Bank of the River 45
Green Side Up 46
One Thing After Another 47
Unnatural Selections: A Meditation upon
    Witnessing a Bullfrog Fucking a Rock 48
Fishing Devil's Hole at the Peak of Spring 51
Getting After It 55
How to Catch the Biggest Fish 56
Hard Work 57
There It Is 58
Knowing When to Stop 59
Vacation Expenses 60
Basic Precepts and Avuncular Advice
    for Young Men 61
Killing 62
Death and Dying 63

New Poems and Short Prose

The Banker 67
The Real Last Words of Billy the Kid 69
The Moving Part of Motion 71
How About 72
Necessary Angels 75
Prayer Bones 76
Magic and Beauty 78
Day Moon 80
Karma Bird 81
The Tunnel 82
Hagerty Wrecks Another Company Truck 84
Obsession 85
Love Find 86
Flux 87
Thanks for the Dance 88
The Stone 89
Woman in a Room Full of Rubber Numbers 90

Reason to Live   91
Scratch   92
Salvage   93
An Epithalamium for Victoria   95
Falling into Place   97
Play-By-Play   98
Job Application   99
The Mouth of the River   100
The Prior and Subsequent Heavens   101
Old Growth   103
Three Ways to Get the Carrot on the Stick   107
Eurydice Ascending   108
The Drought of '76   110
True Account of the Saucer People   111
About Time   112
Smithereens   118
Jack o' Hearts Shopping Mortmart   119
Holy Shit   120

Notes and Acknowledgments

With few exceptions, the selected work in this volume appeared in limited edition letterpress broadsides, cards, and chapbooks published by Jerry Reddan's Tangram Press in Berkeley, California, who also designed this volume. I've worked almost exclusively with Jerry for two decades, always with a sense of privilege, delight, and gratitude.

The first group of poems in this book, from "Learning to Talk" through "Bathing Joe," constitutes annual Winter Solstice cards mailed to friends and colleagues, and also includes a few broadsides and occasional verse.

The poems from "Mahogany China" through "A Firmer Grasp of the Obvious" are selected from *Palms to the Moon*, a loose group of love poems published in 1987 in an edition limited to 100 copies and given away to friends and fellow practitioners.

Bait & Ice, a small gathering of poems on fishing, philosophy, and nature, was released in 1991 in an edition of 175, and includes the poems from "The Work of Art" through "Fishing Devil's Hole at the Peak of Spring."

The final chapbook from which work for this volume was drawn ("Getting After It" through "Death and Dying") is *Piss-Fir Willie Poems*, a suite of persona poems offered as an homage to the vernacular of Pacific northcoast working people, particularly loggers, restoration workers, commercial fishers, ranchers, and those, like my father, in the building trades. I tried to capture the idiom—the diction, cadence, phrasing—as well as that combination of aesthetics, attitude, and turn-of-mind that constitutes cultural style. To my sense of it, I was successful enough that I can't honestly claim the poems as my own. Whatever virtues of language, wit, or wisdom the reader might find, praise should accrue to the speakers from whom I borrowed; any liabilities, alas, are likely mine. *Piss-Fir Willie Poems* was published by Tangram in 1998 in an edition of 200 copies.

Before 1980, I also published two other chapbooks– *da Vaca in a Vanishing Geography* and (with Robert Funt) *Sollla Sollew*–but because these Mad River Press productions were published anonymously and pointedly anti-copyright, I haven't included that work.

New poems, written or substantially revised in the past decade, make up roughly the second half of this volume.

A few of the new and selected works have appeared in other books and journals:

A version of "Green Side Up" was first published in Dalmo'ma VI: *Working the Woods, Working the Sea* (Empty Bowl, 1986) under the title "Treeplanting in the Rain." The poem, under the latter title, was also published in *Paperwork* (Harbour 1991) and *Propriety and Possibilities* (Harrish Press, 1996).

"Aweigh" appeared in *From the Island's Edge: A Sitka Reader* (Graywolf Press, 1995) and *Northcoast View*.

"Unnatural Selections: A Meditation upon Witnessing a Bullfrog Fucking a Rock," "The Banker," and "Mahogany China" were published in *Terra Nova* (Volume 3, Number 4, Fall 1998).

"Hard Work" appeared in *Forest News* (Winter 1999).

"Learning to Talk" and "Bathing Joe" appeared in *Wild Duck Review*, Casey Walker's excellent journal of literature, necessary mischief, and news.

All books are more than the writer's words, and in that spirit I'd like to acknowledge Jerry Reddan for his design of this volume; Pete Stoelzl for his impeccable typesetting; Christopher Stinehour's calligraphic designs; and Shannon Dixon at Proof Positive for his work in helping create the cover. The cover art is the second panel of a triptych from my mentor and friend Morris Graves' *The Great Blue Heron and the Great Rainbow Trout Yogi in Phenomenal Space, Mental Space and the Space of Consciousness* (tempera on paper, 1979), used with the kind permissions of Morris' archive executor Robert Yarber and the Humboldt Arts Council. I also wish to thank the production directors at Grove/Atlantic and Canongate Books, Muriel Jorgensen and Caroline Gorham respectively, as well as the copy editors and art directors involved.

Three bows to Gary Snyder for his usual tough reading of the manuscript and his suggestion for the title.

I also offer special thanks to my editors, Morgan Entrekin at Grove/Atlantic and Jamie Byng of Canongate for their steadfast support of my literary work.

Melanie Jackson, my agent, deserves particular mention for her unstinting efforts and merciful acumen on my behalf.

Finally, my deepest gratitude to family and friends for their unflagging faith, encouragement, and forbearance.

Selected Poems

Short Prose

Learning to Talk

Whenever Jason said "beeber" for "*beaver*"
or "skirl" for "*squirrel*"
I secretly loved it.
They're better words:
The busy beeber beebing around;
the grey squirrel's tail
like a skirl of smoke along a maple branch.
I never told him he was saying
their names "wrong,"
though I did pronounce them conventionally.
One time he noticed, and explained,
" 'Beeber' is how I say it."
"Great," I told him, "whatever
moves you."
But within a week
he was pronouncing both "properly."
I did my duty
and I'm sorry.
Farewell Beeber and Skirl.
So much beauty lost to understanding.

The Cookie Jar

Coddington Mall was clogged with Christmas shoppers as I waited in line at the Cookie Jar, a bakery devoted to my favorite confection.

It was just after noon–lunch break–and a single clerk was left to work the counter, a young woman with a strained, scattered smile. She was working as fast as she could, but the line moved slowly. I was passing the time with the sports page, idly considering whether the 49ers were worth $100 and three points against the Rams, when my attention was drawn to the elderly woman in front of me in line. By her stoop and wrinkles I figured she was in her early 70s, or a hard 65 at least. She was wearing a grey dress, but it was nearly obscured by a heavy black sweater that hung almost to the hemline. She was leaning forward, weight on her cane, her nose to the display case, examining the cookies with the calm, fierce attention of a hawk. Taken by the force of her concentration, I folded the sports page and said pleasantly, "It's always tough to decide."

Her gaze didn't flicker.

I couldn't blame her for ignoring me. Why should an old woman, in a culture of muggers, rapists, and rip-off artists, encourage the idle conversation of some bearded and obviously half-demented hippie from the hills, where he probably grew tons of marijuana and did Lord-knows-what to the sheep. I felt the little wash of sadness that comes when your good intentions are blanked by cultural circumstances. I didn't persist.

When it was the old woman's turn, in a thick Slavic accent she ordered three chocolate chip cookies. "The big ones," she specified, tapping the glass to indicate her choice.

The harried clerk dutifully plucked out three of the saucer-sized cookies with a confectioner's tissue. I noticed one of the cookies had a small chunk broken off its side. So did the old woman: "None that are broke!" she commanded.

The clerk gave her a smile on automatic pilot and replaced the defective cookie, slipping them into a white sack and placing it on the counter. "A dollar-seventy-six please," she told the old woman.

The old woman turned her back to me and began fumbling in her purse, which was the size of a small knitting bag. After much muttering she finally produced two dollar bills rolled together and neatly bound with a yellow rubber band. She addressed the clerk with a staunch formality: "Also I would like some peanut butter cookies. The little ones. Twenty-four cents of them."

The clerk, with a look that pleaded *God, I wish my period would start*, scooped out three small peanut butter cookies and, without bothering to weigh them, slipped them in the bag with the others. The old woman rolled the yellow rubber band off the two bills and spread them out on the counter, pausing to smooth them flat before she secured the white sack in her knitting-bag purse, dropped in the yellow rubber band and the receipt, and left at a brisk shuffle. I lost sight of her in the flow of the crowd as I stepped forward to place my order.

About a half hour later, however, while I was sitting on a bench at the other end of the mall, still pondering the money and points as I polished off a last hot dog, the old woman appeared and, after considerable maneuvering, plopped herself down on the far end of the bench.

Without any acknowledgment of my presence, she opened the white bag from the Cookie Jar. At a bite each, with slow and luscious enjoyment, she ate the three small peanut butter cookies. When she'd finished, she peered into the bag to check the other three, the big ones, and then, as if to confirm their existence, their promise of delight, she named them one by one:

"Friday night.
         Saturday night.
                  Sunday with tea."

Things Thought Through

The path of water is not noticed by water,
but is realized by water. –DŌGEN

Thinking things through.
Thinking through things.
Things through thinking.
Through thinking things.

On Balance

At fifteen,
the imagination
torments;
at fifty,
it consoles.

Another transformation
changing nothing.

Decomposition

I don't know
and I don't know

what to do about it.
I simply hit a point

where I lost heart for judgments
and was swept

into the voluptuous, harrowing complexities
composing a single breath.

Psycho Ecology

An Homage to Walt Whitman

Reality is the work of imagination.
Imagination, the flume of emotion.
After all the tears and laughter,
emotion empties into spirit,
and spirit condenses on reality
like dew on a leaf of grass.

Life of the Spirit

A salmon leaps.
Transcend what?

Aweigh

Vicky and I were steelhead fishing on a secret riffle of a nameless Pacific Northwest river, perhaps the best iron-head water between the Russian and Bella Coola, to which you may receive directions for a thousand dollars cash. It was late afternoon, the sky the color of wet ashes, the river high but beginning to clear. I was drifting a roe-glo through the upper stretch of the run when I felt a slight pause in the *tick-tick-tickity* rhythm of the pencil-lead sinker bouncing along the stony bottom. I set the hook. The rod tip bowed and began to pulse, the heavy, solid throb running through my shoulders.

"Fish on!" I hollered to Vicky forty yards downstream.

She turned and looked at me, yelling back, "Really?"

For some reason, this is the usual response of my fishing companions, leading me to believe they regard me as either an astonishingly inept fisherman or an insanely reckless liar.

"Really!" I assured her at the top of my lungs, lifting my doubled rod as proof before turning my attention to the battle.

Actually, it wasn't much of a battle. The fish was sulking in the strong mid-channel current. I tightened the star drag slightly and applied some pressure; the fish turned lethargically and headed downstream. I lightly thumbed the spool; at the added resistance, the fish swung toward shore down by Vicky, who had just reeled in and started walking my way, no doubt to offer encouragement, counsel, and general assistance.

As my line sliced toward her, she stopped and peered into the water, then shook her head. "Hey," she called, "you've got a big ol' sore-tail salmon."

"No," I begged her.

She pointed emphatically a few feet offshore. "I can *see* it. Big, beat-up sore-tail."

I took the Lord's name in serious vain–no wonder the fish wasn't fighting–then tightened the drag to reel in the fish for quick release. The fish offered little resistance until it was about twenty feet away, then made a sullen move toward swifter water. When I clamped down, it swung back, passing in front of me. Sure enough, it was a spent salmon, its rotting fins worn to nubs, the battered body mottled with patches of dull white fungus.

But something wasn't right. The sore-tail was languidly corkscrewing along the bottom, a movement that didn't match the steady quiver I felt through the rod. Then I saw why: The sore-tail, in blind expression of the spawn-till-you-die imperative, was engaged in a last-gasp courtship of the fish actually connected to my line, a steelhead longer than a yardstick and as deep as a Dutch oven.

Hearing Vicky move up behind me, I whispered, "That sore-tail you saw isn't the fish I have on. It's trailing my fish, which is one humongous *hog* of a steelie, putting on some spawning moves."

"Sure it is," Vicky said.

I worked the steelhead a few feet closer, telling Vicky without turning my head, "Step up easy and see for yourself."

Vicky stepped up easy, very easy, but not easy enough.

The riffle was about fifty yards wide. With the power of a nitro-fueled dragster, the steelie crossed it in one second flat, leaving me blinded by the mist sprayed from the spool mingled with smoke from the drag. Struck dumber than usual, I simply stood there as the whopper steelie made a sharp right at the opposite shore and streaked downstream. I watched the line melting from the spool. I felt like my nervous system was being stripped from my body through my solar plexus, a rush beyond sensation toward something as clean and empty as my spool was about to be if I didn't stop the fish. But I didn't want to stop the fish. I didn't want the feeling to end.

The spool was almost down to the backing when the steelie abruptly swung back into the heavy current and dove to the bottom, slowly lashing its head.

I wanted to tell Vicky to go home and pack some grub because I was going to be there all night, but when I finally got my slack jaw working I discovered I couldn't utter the few words I could remember.

Train wreck in the cerebellum. Synaptic bridges collapsed.

I concentrated on the basic sounds, managing something close to "Biffeegaaaagh."

Vicky cocked her head. "You what?"

"Big," I gasped. "Godzilla."

At the moment, though, it felt more like I was hooked to Godzilla's heart, thirty pounds of pure throbbing force, the rainbowed rod pulsing steadily as the fish hung in the current, gathering power for another slashing run.

Then the hook pulled out.

I felt like a lover had just hung up the phone after telling me, "I'm sorry, but it's over."

Like I do when the Dream Joker whispers, "You won 100 million in tonight's lottery," and I wake up broke as usual.

Unplugged a heartbeat short of Divinity, a nanosecond shy of Solid Full Circuit. Lost. Looted and left behind. Mentally exhausted, emotionally gutted, spiritually bereft.

Vicky helped me back to the car.

But as I fell asleep that night, I remembered the wild power of the steelhead's cross-river run, remembered it from my bones out, in nerve-meat and blood, that rush of glory as I emptied into the connection, joined for a moment, each other's ghost, then blown away like mist on the wind. And my gratitude for that moment's nexus overwhelmed the despair of its loss–as if one can truly possess or lose anything, or the connection ever break.

In fishing, as the moment of experience enters the future as memory, it's prey to seizures of enlargement and general embellishing. I feel sure, however, that that steelhead weighed close to twenty-eight pounds. It's possible–and, given a few more years of voluptuous recollection, almost certain–that the fish would have tipped the Toledoes at over thirty, making it easily conceivable that I'd hooked what would have been a new state-record steelie. But even taking the distortions of time and memory into account, ruthlessly pruning any possibility of exaggeration, carefully considering the Parallax Effect, the Water Magnification Variable, the Wishful Thinking Influence, and the El Feces del Toro Predilection, I would lay *even* money in the real world that that steelhead weighed at least twenty-six pounds, and would gladly wager a new car of your choice against a soggy cornflake that it was twenty-four minimum.

In that spirit, I trust you will understand that I offer a blessing when I wish for our coming years that a big one always gets away.

Tao-to-Tao

The way is
The way it is
Because that's the way
It is,
And why.

To Be

ODE

Loins and breath.

Moonlight melting
In the throat of a calla lily.

Thickets of young maple
Just breaking bud.

All you have to be
Is who you are,

Naked beyond the body,
A touch at a time.

PALINODE

*All you have to be
Is who you are?*
What could have I possibly
Meant by that

If part of you
Is who you dream you could be
If you weren't the piddling little dimwit
You actually are,

As if the "real you"
Is the one who sits around wondering who
The real you is—

Or if you've ever wished you were
Someone else, anybody–

An accountant in Coronado,
A dishwasher in a second-rate Omaha steakhouse–

Or if you can follow this,
Or still care,
You're probably really screwed up

Or close enough
To be welcomed as a friend.

Practice, Practice, Practice

It exacts the strictest discipline
To truly take it easy

Yet still retain the minimal
Quiver of ambition
Required for consciousness.

That's what I've been working on all morning,

Stretched out on the couch
By the cabin window at Bob's,

Watching the rain,
Without pattern,
Fall on the pond,

Just me and the dogs.

Wisdom and Happiness

The wet crescents left by the dogs' tongues
licking spilled cat kibble from the cabin floor;

the strand of light, finer than spider-spun,
unspooling from the center of my chest
as a 20-pound steelhead slashes downstream
through the celadon waters of the Smith;

the gleam of water on Victoria's flanks
in that moment of stepping
from the sauna into a wild Pacific storm—
vapor-wreathed shimmer, body gone;

the elegance of an elk track
cut in sandy streamside silt;

red alder bud-break in early March;

venison stew and fresh salmon,
garden corn coming on;

Jason asleep on a school night,
his bare right leg dangling from the bed
(geez, he's getting big);

sliding a chunk of madrone
into the firebox on a snowy night,
damping the wood heater down
for coals to kindle the morning's fire;

the way the terriers sneeze and leap and race
deliriously through the orchard
when they know we're going on a walk;

raindrops still cupped in huckleberry leaves
hours after the rain has stopped:

I made 55 years today, still hanging on,
and though only fools lay claim to wisdom
I don't know what else to call it
when every year
it takes less to make me happy,
and it lasts longer.

Red Sails

I sit at my desk
and for no apparent reason
start singing, badly,
Red sails in the sunset . . .
sing it until I sail out of myself,
whatever a self is,
crazier than shit,
you bet,
and deeply grateful.

Squall & Commotion

You've reached bottom
when you understand
there is no bottom
to reach.
And just rock there drenched
on the ship's bow,
watching the rain
fall on the ocean.

Slow Learner

Know the plants.
        —GARY SNYDER

It's been 50 years, most oblivious, but now,
if only in glimpses, I can look at plants
and feel the light composing them.

Falling asleep, I comfort myself
with a little prayer of their names:
alder, larkspur, thimbleberry, salal.

Bathing Joe

AN ELEGY FOR BOB, 1946–1994

The summer of '94 at French Flat, on a scorching after-
noon in mid-July, my brother Bob suggested we bathe
his dog Joe, a sixteen-year-old Kelpie. Since Bob held
intractably to the notion that bathing dogs more than
once a year destroys their essential skin oils, I hustled to
gather the leash, towels, and doggie shampoo before he
changed his mind.

Joe–112 in human years–truly needed a bath. He
suffered every affliction of elderly canines: deaf as dirt;
a few glimmers short of blind; lumpy with warts and
subcutaneous cysts; a penis pointing straight down; a
scrotum so saggy his testicles banged against his hocks;
prone to drool; given to a seemingly constant flatulence
that would be banned under the Geneva Accords; and
possessed of what the genteel call "doggie odor," which
in Joe's unfortunate case ranged between gaggingly rank
and living putrefaction. When Joe dozed by the wood-
heater on a winter's eve, enjoying dinner was difficult–
considering one's watering eyes and the instinct to cover
the food.

So I had the leash on Joe before Bob, whose right
leg had been amputated near the hip years earlier, could
get up on his crutches. With Bob herding from behind,
I led Joe around back of the cabin, where we'd set up
an old bathtub for starlit soaks. We hadn't used the
bathtub lately, so I scooped out the accumulated litter
of madrone leaves and pine needles before I lifted in
Joe. As I slipped off his collar, Joe grunted and sat
down, settling into what we called the ODZ, or Old
Dog Zone, where Joe seemed to be watching methane
sunsets on Jupiter, or flights of birds invisible to human
eyes. I turned on the water, hot and cold mixing in

a single hose, while Bob opened the shampoo.

I asked him, "Want me to put in the plug?"

"Jesus, no," Bob said. "Rising water freaks Joe out bad. In fact, better make sure that drain ain't clogged."

"How could it be?" I reminded him. "Remember when you couldn't find the rubber plug one night and hammered in that chunk of redwood for a stopper? Knocked out all those little cross-pieces?"

"Aw," Bob dismissed the memory, "they were rusted all to shit anyway. Besides, the tub drains on the ground–not like there's a pipe to clog." He squirted some shampoo on his palm. "You gonna stand there yakking or are we gonna get on it–it's broiling out here."

Joe returned from Jupiter when the stream of water hit him. He bolted for safety but couldn't get traction on the tub's slick bottom. Bob grabbed him around the neck and Joe slid to the front of the tub. He held still, warbling softly as I soaked him down.

"It's okay, Joe, you're okay," Bob comforted his pooch, working the shampoo into a grey lather. Joe struggled again, scrambling to get his back legs under him, then suddenly stopped. His yellowish dingo eyes began to widen.

"Brain-lock," I opined.

Bob ignored me to encourage Joe: "Good dog, good dog. Just keep still and we'll be done in a few minutes. You can't help being old, can you?"

Joe answered with a low, trembling yowl.

"What's he yodeling about?" I wondered aloud.

"Hell if I know." Bob rubbed Joe's neck. "What's the matter buddy?"

I noticed the greyish-yellow scum building in the bath-tub and gratuitously advised Bob, "I wouldn't bathe that dog without some industrial-strength, eight-ply latex gloves. You wake up tomorrow, you might not have fingernails."

Bob glanced at the rising scum. "*That's* the problem. Joe's sitting on the drain, got it blocked, and the water's rising–thinks he's gonna drown. Let me scoot him back down, off the drain."

But when Bob tried to slide him toward the middle of the tub, Joe's yowl leaped an octave and he twisted his head free of Bob's grasp. Joe huddled against the front curve of the tub, a strong shiver passing through him from flank to nose.

I turned off the water. "Now what?"

"Beats me," Bob declared, then cooed at Joe, "What's your problem, buddy? You're not gonna drown." Bob slipped his hand underwater and felt beneath Joe. When he withdrew his hand he gave me a funny look. "You're not gonna believe this," he said solemnly, "but Joe's got his nuts caught in the drain."

"Impossible," I assured him. "The drain's too small for his nuts to fit through."

Bob shook his head. "Maybe not if they were soapy and slid through one at a time. Better take a look under there. I'll hold Joe."

The tub was set about eight inches off the ground on a wooden frame, so I had to brace both legs and lift with a shoulder to rock the tub back far enough to see. Sure enough, Joe's testicles were dangling from the drain, side by side in his flaccid, mottled scrotum.

Bob took a break from consoling his dog to ask, "See anything?"

I eased the tub back down. "Yeh, I see your dog's nuts caught in the drain. I trust you appreciate my reluctance to believe it."

"Well," Bob said impatiently, "try to poke them back through. Ol' Joe's about to go into shock."

Joe whimpered piteously in confirmation.

"You're kidding," I said. "Try to '*poke them back through*.' Hey bro, he's *your* dog and those are *his* nuts–

you do it. Poking Joe's stuck nuts is not even *on* my list of 25,000 things I'd do for fun or money."

"Sweet Jesus," Bob sighed with pained exasperation, "show class or show ass."

I'd forgotten that Bob, with only one leg, probably couldn't leverage the tub, so I gracefully offered, "*I'll* lift the tub; *you* handle his nuts."

"Ah, come on," Bob objected, "someone's got to hold Joe. If he panics, he'll either tear them off or stretch his sack so bad his balls will be bouncing along behind him the rest of his life." He scratched Joe's head, murmuring, "Hang on, old pal, we'll get you loose."

I had an idea. "Maybe we could take a sledgehammer to the tub—sort of break it out around him."

"Right, good thinking," Bob mocked me. "Take a twelve-pound sledge to a metal bathtub. We'd have him loose by next month easy." He shook his head. "How would you like *your* nuts caught in the drain and some utter dimwit pounding away on the tub with a sledge-hammer?"

"All right," I said, "but it'll cost you."

"Why doesn't that surprise us?" Bob asked his dog. Then to me, "What?"

"Dishes for a week plus that little Shimano reel you hardly ever use anyway."

Bob explained to Joe, "You're gonna be here a long time, buddy, because my brother is a no-class, show-ass jerk."

Swabbing sweat off my brow, too hot for prolonged negotiations, I surrendered. "Hand me that damn bottle of shampoo."

I lifted the tub again, sweat-blind in the heat, and awkwardly squirted some shampoo on Joe's scrotum for lubrication. Taking a deep breath, I began working Joe's testicles around in his sack, trying to arrange them vertically for a push upward, all the while providing a running commentary on my feelings for Bob's amusement and to deflect all but essential attention from the task at hand: "Forty-nine years I've been alive. Representing the present culmination of millennia of species evolution. Of exacting natural selection. Years of formal education. Diligent study. Developing skills. The long, excruciating refinement of sensibility. And now I understand my whole life has been a preparation for this moment: trying to get your dog's nuts unstuck from a bathtub drain. And I don't know if that's perfect or pathetic or both or none of the above."

"Well," Bob offered with a dry sweetness, "for sure it's better than something worse." Then to Joe, "Listen to him snivel."

I saved my breath and, working by touch, manipulated Joe's nuts around till they were stacked, then, using sort of a reverse milking move, squeezed his scrotum from the bottom. The top testicle popped through, then the other. Joe was free. With an agility he hadn't shown in years, he leaped from the tub and started rolling in the dirt, moaning.

Bob smiled. "There you go, buddy! Happy dog!"

When I dropped the tub off my numb shoulder, the dirty water sluiced forward and slopped over the rim, drenching me.

I sniveled some more: "Oh great, I free his worthless old nuts and what do I get—soaked with mutagenic Joe scuzz."

Bob laughed. "Plus you get our eternal gratitude—don't forget that."

I won't.

Mahogany China

My grandmother tells me
About her first love
Johnny Hansen was his name
She'll always remember
A warm autumn day
She was fifteen
Or almost fifteen
Had a mare named Patches
And she and Johnny went riding together
Down along the Chetco River
Low and mossy before the rains.
She can still taste the fried chicken
She made for their picnic
And how worried she was
Her lips would be all greasy
If he wanted to kiss her.

Tells me this as she polishes
The mahogany china closet
Over and over
Five minutes
The same spot
Till it shines.

The First Cut Is the Deepest

Nipples hard
in the chill dusk air,
she stood hip-deep in the Mad River,
pointing as a Great Blue Heron
lifted ungainly from the riffle above
and flew downstream toward the mouth.

We made love all night on the shore,
eager with each other, wild,
fierce and sweet
in those first permissions,
stunned, possessed.

Married, three children,
a ranch above the river,
still able to delight each other with who we were—
that's all I ever really wanted.

Half-sunken, half-emerged,
she points as the Heron flies, as its shadow
folds with the copper shadows of nightfall.

I build a fire on the bank and wait.
Tired, silent, the children go down

and wash their faces in the river.

Waiting for Houdini to Come Up

Magic is not the manipulation of appearance.
It is the expropriation of the real.
Not mastered sleights blurred with patter
but the actual rabbit in every hat.
No tricks. Not the key to the shackles
from her mouth to his
passed in a good-luck kiss
just before they chain him in the trunk
and drop it in the cold, real river.
Not the key, but the kiss itself,
tender, fearful,
as wild as the release within us
when he floats out of the weighted trunk
and from the river bottom begins to rise,
escaping the skilled deceit,
freed from the illusion of escape.

The Countessa

Last night I made love to my passionate countessa
as the Panonia Express
flashed by villages we only saw
as shivers of light
on the green enameled roof of the sleeping car.
Gone an undreamable distance beyond
that first kiss in Budapest,
nearly to Prague,
flaying the moon
as Czechoslovakia slipped under our bodies,
our moans sweetened the iron clatter
of rail and wheel
as we melted with pleasure.
When I woke at the Berlin station
she was gone.
She left a piece of ivory
curled in my hand.

Destroyed by strength
as much as weakness.
By the ravishing, bare-back, fantastic countessa,
by Guinevere, Mary, the moon,
the love invented against loneliness,
the heart exhausted by the mind.
Destroyed by the translucence
at the tip of a root.
The sound of a cello in an empty hall.
By what you can give and what you can take.
Lost by imagining what we cannot know
and knowing what we cannot have.
Believing love will bear us away
down the River of Babylon
to the rumored garden lush with pears.

Wanting it all at once,
the journey consumed
in a blaze of moonlight and dream
so pure even the ashes burn
into the color of her camisole.

And we, as if we'd been denied,
are left wanting even more.
The warmth of her body barely alive
in the piece of ivory curled in our hands.

Venison Stew

FOR FREEMAN HOUSE

I could grow old with you, Freeman,
two woodrats drunk half the time
in a shack way up the Klamath,
with not much left to do
but complain about our teeth and livers,
wonder where the money went,
and watch the river move.
Once a month, if we can beat
another old pickup into running,
we'll clatter down to Eureka for supplies,
maybe give them kids some gambling lessons
and the Humboldt coeds a hopeful tumble.

Two weeks later, still recovering,
I can see you give the cookpot
a slow, appraising stir,
nodding with a resignation so deep
it's joyful,
"Venison stew again."
Spoons scraping the wooden bowls,
we eat in front of the fireplace,
jawing about this and that:
how many gut-busting stones
we lugged for the hearth;
why the salmon are late this year;
the relative merits of Huskies and McCullochs;
the continuing decline of the novel;
why Ann left Willy back in '88;
how on a freezing Skagit Valley morning once
we saw a flock of two hundred geese
wheel above us and turn into snow.

And the days go by like the stories and river
into whatever comfort we deserve.
We eat the stew, laughing.
And the days go by like the sun and moon,
gloriously indifferent
to us crazy old men full of lies,
gumming venison as we slowly grow
helpless and forgetful,
retelling the old stories to keep them new,
till after many meals
the wooden bowl wears through.

Winter Song

IN MEMORY OF DOROTHY MILLIMAN

The acceptance of death
Clear down in our hearts
Is the faith we bring to life
That love may go on:

The lustrous umber
Of decaying ferns;
Belled vermilion
Of the gooseberry bloom;

Rain on the river.

On Humor: On Mating Donkeys and Onions

When you cross donkeys with onions
mainly you get a lot of onions with big ears.

That's the first part of the joke.
The silliness language invites,
the aimless
consequence of play
when you're just playing around
plucking this and that
out of endless possibilities
and putting them together.
The mind fucking off for the afternoon.
Fun, you bet, but
not essential;
and not really what you'd hoped for
crossing donkeys and onions
the only way they can be crossed–
in minds wild enough to join them
just to see
what happens.

And what happens
is you mainly get
onions with big ears.
But love invariably rewards imagination,
so every once in a while you get
a piece of ass
that brings tears to your eyes.

Watering the Garden
on the Hottest Day of the Summer

Hey, Fence Lizard!
Think it's gonna rain?

Heh-eh-eh:
You were wrong.

Palms to the Moon

I

We were fifteen. Summertime.
We walked through the moonlit village
to the cliffs above the beach.
We made love at that trembling pitch
where sensations become emotions,
none of which we'd ever felt before.
Our hearts like torches hurled into the sea.
A magnificence
that cannot survive
the innocence
that makes it possible.

2

No beauty without perishing.
No love without that first desolate moment of heartbreak
when you know something is wrong,
but you don't know what it is,
or how to stop it.

3

Midnight, the mountains,
we make a bed of our clothes
on the granite slab.
Naked beyond skin,
we lift our palms to the moon,
our bodies trembling like the limb of a tree
a heartbeat after the bird has flown.

A Firmer Grasp of the Obvious

Evening, early June,
sweetly tired from the day's work,
lazed out on the back porch with friends,
just finished with dinner
(asparagus and spinach fresh from the garden;
venison backstrap
smoky and rare),

watching the sunset
luster the ocean,
stiff-winged swifts
etching the air,
a full moon rising like a fever of pearl
huge above the redwoods,

I'm seized by the realization
I'll never understand
the origin and destination of the universe,
the meaning or purpose of life,
none of the answers
to the great questions of being,
and probably not much else.

And that knowledge, at last,
making me happy.

The Work of Art

The only essential creation
Is a life that gives you life.
Figure you're doing real good
When all you need
Is bait and ice.

Steelhead Fishing, Smith River, January

So cold I'm sure I'd piss snowflakes
before my plumbing froze.
So cold the guides on my Lamiglass
freeze between casts, forcing me
to dip the rod in the warmer river
to melt them clear
for another futile cast and drift
from the quick head of the riffle
down through the slow fan of the tail-out.
So in-fucking-credibly cold
that under the latest-miracle-fabric thermals,
layers of wool,
and insulated waders with thick socks,
I'm shivering like a chipmunk shitting marbles—
so close to total loss of motor control
I finally open to the obvious:
For what possible reason
am I risking hypothermia, frostbite, and further
        brain damage
if not to hook a sea-run rainbow trout,
albeit one so numbed by icy water
it would be like snagging a sand-packed boot?

I can imagine many fine and sufficiently crazy answers,
but the truth is I don't know.
The more philosophical might suggest
perhaps I'm really fishing
for the real reason I fish,
but that's too many mirrors and French intellectuals
for me to survive short of twisted.
But if reason exists this side of insanity,
I suspect it's simple and deep:

faith refreshed through flowing water;
the opalescent cascade of trout mating;
the way my heart flies open
when a sea-bright rainbow
slashes into a downstream run;
the salt-minted shimmer of divinity as it leaps.

The Third Bank of the River

The three deer drinking
in the moonlit shallows across the river
snap alert.

Muzzles dripping,
ears flared tense,
shiver of flanks as muscles coil

into that trembling poise
between stillness and flight,
they listen to my heartbeat

till I hear it myself.

Green Side Up

*Kid, there's only two things a tree planter needs to know:
the green side goes up, and ain't no raingear in the world
that'll keep you dry.*
                    —Piss-Fir Willie

Once you're soaked
It doesn't matter
If it's raining.

The trees go in
One by one by one
And you go on

Borne and lost in
The mindless rhythm,
Bent to the task.

No time at all
You forget the rain,
Blur into its

Monotony.
Between root and breath,
No difference—

It's all hard work.
Your wet body burns
From the bones out.

One Thing After Another

So many true paths.
A wealth of exceptional teachers.
Countless rivers I've never fished.
Love's possibilities defying math.
All these dirty dishes.

Unnatural Selections: A Meditation upon Witnessing a Bullfrog Fucking a Rock

Amalgam of electric jelly,
constellated neural knots
in the briny binary soup,
as surely as stimulus prods response
brains are made to choose.
And through a major error in pattern recognition
or a significant cognitive fault,
the bullfrog's brain has selected
a two-pound rock
as the object of his rampant affection,
a rock (to my admittedly mammalian eye)
that neither resembles
nor even vaguely suggests
the female of his species.

He does seem to be enjoying himself
in a blunted sort of way,
but since the rock so obviously remains unmoved
one suspects it's not the blending of sweet oblivions
that fuels his persistence,
but a serious kink in a feedback loop—
or perhaps just kinkiness in general.
The less compassionate might even call him
the quintessentially insensitive male.

Assuming a pan-species gender bond
and a common fret,
I advise my amphibious pal,
"Hey, I don't think she's *playing* hard to get.
That's the literal case you're up against, Jack—
true story, buddy; stone fact.
And I'd be fraternally remiss if I didn't share

my deep and eminently reasonable doubt
that she'll be worn down
however long and spectacular the ardor."

Ignoring my counsel
as completely as he has my presence,
the bullfrog continues his fruitless assault
with that brain-locked commitment to folly
which invariably accompanies
dumb, bug-eyed lust.

But, in fairness,
whose brain hasn't shorted out in a slosh of hormones
or, igniting like a shattered jug of gas,
fireballed into a howling maelstrom
where a rock indeed might seem a port?
One can only conclude
that such impelling concupiscence
serves as a species' life insurance,
sort of a procreative override
of any decision requiring thought,
thought being notoriously prey to thinking,
and the more one thinks about thinking
the thinkier it gets.
Therefore, though the brain is made to choose,
its very existence ultimately depends
on the generative supremacy of brainless desire—
for with all respect to Monsieur Descartes
you am before you can think you are.
Dirt-drive compulsions riding powerful desires
render any choice moot, along with
reason, morality, taste, manners,
and all those other jars of glitter
we pour on the sticky and raw.

The hard truth is we never chose to choose:

not the brains we use to pick
between competing explanations for our sexual mess
nor these hearts we've burdened with our blunders
in the name of love.
Do whatever we decide we will,
the choice isn't free;
we live at the mercy of more pressing needs.

Thus, urges urgently surging,
we mount a few rocks by mistake.
A bit more embarrassing than most of our
        foolishness, true—
but so what?
The power of the imperative
coupled with the law of averages
virtually guarantees enough will get it right
to make more brains to be made up
about exactly what steps to take
toward what we think we need to do
on this stony journey between delusion and mirage—
when to move, how to use our dreams—
a journey where we finally learn
freedom is not a choice
a brain is free to choose.

Fortunately, my warty friend,
the soul is built to cruise.

Fishing Devil's Hole at the Peak of Spring

From the top of Temple Ridge
to the South Fork of the Gualala
it's all downhill,

the first half-mile so steep
I wouldn't have time for a decent scream
before splattering against
one of the redwoods whose tops loom below,

a remnant stand of old-growth
the terrain has spared from logging.
Praying it will spare me too,
I descend

carefully, carefully, feet
planted sideways,
waving my rod case for balance

like some moronic progeny
of Izaak Walton and a Flying Wallenda,
work my way, stab and dig,

down and then some into Devil's Hole,
utterly certain which orifice
inspired the gorge's name,
just as certain there must be an easier way;
down till the slope finally relents,

relatively gentles
as I pass through the trees,
their vibrant new-growth glossy in the early light,

then down easy
and across the alluvial terrace meadow
clotted with sun-cups, poppies, blue-eyed grass,
purple blooms of wild iris
lurid as a pornographer's sense of romance;

down to the river.
                    Sneakers and Levi's,
I wade right in, flicking
a Gold-ribbed Hare's Ear I tied myself
to the riffle above the pool,

following it as it sinks,
bellies with the flow,
drifts . . .
my mind drifting beyond it,

downstream where the durable curve of water
has undercut an azalea-shaded bank,
and I'm trying to imagine what swoon of fragrance
        might be loosed
from the light-drenched flowers
when the sun touches them about three hours from now,

and wondering whether it would be wise to wait
or better just to imagine and move on,
so when the trout strikes I miss it by five minutes,
and despite a dozen delicate, dedicated casts,
damned if I can bring him again.

No matter. It's a magnificent morning,
three miles of river to my climb-out at the bridge,
and if that azalea cut-bank isn't a lunker's dream home
I don't know diddly about fishing
and should give it up on the spot–

chuck my rod in this emerald pool
and devote myself hereafter
to scholarly articles on Norwegian grammar,
lavishing on the future-conditional tense
passion now reserved for luring fish into the present.

When I turn to wade the rocky shallows
back to better footing on the gravelly river-bar,
a nervous frog I hadn't noticed at my feet
decides this dawdling critter
may be as clumsy as he is lost

and so for dear life leaps—
a flat-out half-yard sprawling flop
that stuns him a floating moment
before he jackknifes, ass in air, and dives,
digs down till his belly scrapes bottom,

then kicks away rhythmically through the clear shallows,
puffs of stirred-up silt, evenly spaced, billowing
        in his wake.
And watching those milky silica clouds
bloom and disperse,
                swirl and settle,

a force summoned by the footloose glory of the day,
something wild within me,
something I like to think of as poetry
presses for release,
and I say aloud to hear it myself,

"So this is what my life has come to:
a fierce sweetness in the river light;
delirious fusion of petal and flesh,
plunge and glide."

Thus lost in exaltation, mindlessly
I step on an algae-slimed rock,
hang in baffled contemplation
of my sky-framed sneakers dripping on my face,

then smack ass
into the cold, marrow-shriveling water.

"Yarrrrrgggggggggaaaaaahhhhhhhhhhh!"

Yes. Yes by everything holy, *yes*!
Even better.

Getting After It

All the planters on our crew
Packed double tree-bags.
Piss-Fir Willie harnessed three,
And stuffed another 20 bare-root stock
In a day-pack with his lunch.
When Timothy ragged him one morning–
"Geez, Willie, you could probably get
Another six down each pants leg
And a dozen between your teeth"–

Willie turned to him and said,
Loud enough for us all to hear,
"I'll tell you what my daddy told me:
Son, if you're gonna be a bear,
Be a grizzly."

How to Catch the Biggest Fish

Pouring December rain, the crummy's windows
    all steamed up,
Our tree-planting crew was talking salmon fishing
    during lunch
When Piss-Fir Willie matter-of-factly announced,
"Due to my natural modesty I didn't mention it
    to you boys,
But I caught me a 30-pound chinook on
    Thanksgiving morn—
Hit a big silver spinner in the Ten-Ten Hole."
J-Root Johnny immediately hooted, "Hey, dude,
Throw that fucking minnow back!
I nailed one in the gorge last week
That went 38—" But before we could ask him on what
(A pitchfork was rumored his favorite lure)
Pete Tucker honked, "Put it in Glad Bag, Johnny,
And set it out on the curb. I landed one
From that little pool behind the Ulrick Ranch
That weighed-out a hair over 42
On the Hiouchi Hamlet scales."
At which Willie threw up his hands and wailed,
"Shitfire! On this damn crew
The first liar don't have a chance."

Hard Work

Boys, I've listened to your horseshit enough.
You want to know what hard work is, listen up:
I've rode a misery whip; carried hod;
Pulled green-chain; broke big rocks into little rocks;
Whupped a hundred miles of picket fence;
Set choker in country so rough
You were doing good if you could crawl downhill.
I've fought wildfire; lugged sandbags against floods;
Bucked hay till I was tripping on my tongue;
And made so damn much split stuff
I plumb wore out a sledgehammer head
And a couple o' pairs of elk-hide gloves.
So you boys can write it down as gospel when I tell you
The hardest work you'll find in this world
Is digging the grave for someone you loved.

There It Is

They can do
Whatever you
Can't stop them
From doing.
You can do
Whatever you
Can pull off
And still live
With yourself.

Knowing When to Stop

You've had too much
When you can't remember
How much you've had
And wouldn't give a rat's ass
If you could.

Vacation Expenses

Back from his annual two-week vacation in Petaluma,
I notice Willie is slow with his shovel
As we set a gate post at the south end of Temple Flat.
I kid him, "What's the matter, Willie, you forget
How to run that Irish backhoe in the big city?"
And though he snaps back, "Shit, I *wore out*
More shovels before I had a hair on my ass
Than you're likely to use in your whole life,"
For Willie the response is halfhearted,
And he does seem to be moving a little sore.
"Feeling puny?" I inquire.
"A bit," he allows.
Tamps some more rock around the post,
Then leans on the shovel handle like a Caltrans worker
And gazes across the flat into the brown summer hills.
"You know," he shakes his head,
"A man's plumb crazy to ever go to town.
First nine days of vacation I spent drinking whiskey,
Then spent about five minutes getting the ever-living shit
Stomped out of me by some Mexican field workers
I pissed off in a South Street bar.
Then I spent most of the night in the drunk tank
        pissing blood
Before they yarded me over to County Hospital
Where I spent the rest of my vacation.
Figure $500 on whiskey, a grand on fines,
And another $4700 for them fucking hospital bills.
Them Mexican fellers might have stomped me stupid,
But I ain't dumb. Here on out,
I'm taking my vacations twenty minutes at a time,
Right here in the hills,
Just like I'm doing now."

Basic Precepts and Avuncular Advice
for Young Men

Don't eat a roadkill you can bounce into your pickup.

Don't bare-ass the Highway Patrol.

Long odds on short money is usually a loser.

Don't confuse the gospel with the church.

Never snitch on family or friends.

Avoid living any place where you can't take a piss
    off the front porch.

Just because it's simple doesn't make it easy.

Don't write a check with your 'gator mouth
    that your lizard ass can't cash.

If you don't want her, don't whistle.

Don't get between two dogs kicking dirt.

Anybody can mash potatoes; takes a chef to make gravy.

You're never too poor to pay attention.

Don't mumble around paranoids.

Never sleep with a woman who is doing you a favor.

If you're struck by a bully, turn the other cheek. If he
    whacks you again, shoot the sumbitch.

Keeping it is always twice as difficult as getting it.

Never drive through a small town at 100 mph
    with the sheriff's drunk fifteen-year-old daughter
    naked on your lap.

Never draw against the drop.

If you're not confused, you don't know what's going on.

Love is always harder than it feels.

Killing

Only two ways
You can justify
Killing a critter:

If you're aiming to eat it,
Or it's fixin' to eat you.

Death and Dying

Don't matter diddly
When, where,
Or how
You die.
Important thing is,
Don't take it personal.

New Poems

Short Prose

The Banker

His smile is like a cold toilet seat.
He shakes my hand as if he's found it
floating two weeks dead in a slough.
I tell him I need money.
Tons of it.
I want to buy a new Lamborghini,
load it with absinthe and opium,
and hit the trail out of these rainy hills
for a few years in Paris.
I try to explain
I'm at that point in my artistic development
where I require a long period
of opulent reflection.

The banker rifles my wallet.
Examines my mouth.
Chuckles when I offer 20 Miltonic sonnets
as security on the loan.
Now he's shaking his head, my confidence,
my hand good-bye. "Wait," I plead,
"I have debts and dreams
my present cash flow can't possibly sustain."
"Sorry," he mumbles, "nothing I can do,"
and staples some papers
in a way that makes me feel
he'd rather nail my tongue to an ant hill.
I stare at him in disbelief.

And under the righteous scathing of my gaze
the banker begins to change form.
First, he becomes a plate of cold french fries
drenched in crankcase oil.

Then a black spot
on a page of Genesis.
Finally, a dung beetle,
rolling little balls of shit
across a desk bigger than my kitchen.

Yet even as I follow these morbid transformations
I never lose sight of his bloated face,
the green, handled skin
shining like rotten meat.

But then his other faces
open to mine:
father, lover, young man, child—
our shared human history
folding us into one.
And only that stops me
from beating him senseless
with a sock full of pennies.

The Real Last Words of Billy the Kid

Billy the Kid you can't hide out
inside yourself forever.
Beautiful
twisted killer,
shoot a man dead for looking at him wrong,
even a couple of women some said,
in cold twisted blood
as if the flat burning path of a bullet
straightened anything out.

Sheriff Pat Garrett gunned Billy down
on the dark porch of a bordertown cabin
where Billy, knife in hand,
had gone outside to slice a steak
from a hanging slab of venison,
leaving his lady for the night
asleep inside.

Garrett calling his name just before he pulled the trigger–
"Billy"–
calling him softly.

In the book Garrett wrote about it
he claimed Billy's last words were "¿Quien es"
("Who is it?")
though he privately told his drinking buddies
the real last words of Billy the Kid
were "Ah, shit!"
but the Sheriff hadn't wanted to offend
genteel readers.

"Billy."
Called his name softly out of the darkness
    then blew him away.
The knife clattering on the porch.
The heavy, glazed mass of the deer meat
swaying in the cool night air.
The woman inside beginning to scream.

The Moving Part of Motion

The last of the high plains drifters
canters his palomino through the Montana grain fields,
shockwave ripples undulating in his trampled wake.
The sun burns like magnesium;
the moon like a knot of pitch.
Every movement in the motion he makes
hurts his fractured cheekbone
and the broken hand he holds against his chest.
Pistol-whipped and stomped by the
  psycho Sheriff of Cheyenne
and his Deputies of Derangement,
the drifter, in a thoughtful mood, drifts west-northwest,
where he loosely reckons Missoula is,
thinking it may be time to settle down and marry,
maybe have some kids.
But for now he's simply glad
he made it out of Wyoming alive,
and that his destination is stationary.

How About

FOR JASON STOCKLEY DODGE

All day, relentless,
Jason, just turned six,
captures me in play:
    How about if I'm Jean-Luc Picard
    Commander of the starship *Enterprise*
    and you're Q,
    that mischievous guy who knows everything
    and just sort of popped out of a black hole;
    and a bunch of Cardassians and maybe some
        space monsters
    have locked on to us with a tractor-beam
    and are pulling us into a gamma transducer
    that's robbing our power–
    oh no, our shields are down to 60%!–
    and let me tell you
    our butts are in *trouble*,
    so how about this time–just *once*–
    can we set our phasers on KILL?

Or how about
    I'm Rin-Tin-Tin
    and I'm running through the woods
and how about
    you're a bad guy,
    a real mean criminal,
    and you go hide behind that fir tree
    and you shoot Rinty when he runs by
    and Rinty rolls and rolls down this hill like
        he's dead,
    and just lies there,
    very, very, very still,
    but the thing is

you missed,
Rinty is faking, he fooled you,
and when you walk over
Rinty attacks *Rar-rar-rarrrrrr!*
and you try to shoot him
but Rinty crunches your arm
so you shoot yourself instead and stagger around
until you just fall over deader than a doorknob.
How about that?

Or how about
you're just walking along dah-de-dah
and you see these two little dinosaurs
caught in this basketball net
so you call 911–
and I am Rescue 911–
and I send a fire truck with a ladder and Fireman
    Bob driving with his dog Chief on the back,
plus I send an ambulance,
and I better send another fire truck,
and Fireman Bob rescues the little dinosaurs
and rushes them to the hospital with the siren on–
and how about you're the doctor
but you've never operated on baby dinosaurs before
so I have to show you how
and I fix up their spinal cords and their little hearts
and they're OK now; they're gonna be fine . . .

Until I want to yell
    HOLD IT! STOP!
How about
    if I'm Lothario the Magnificent,
    an alchemist magician,
    and I can focus my wild imagination so powerfully
    I'm able to condense all the women I've ever loved
    into one?

And how about I can imagine with such passionate
        clarity
    that she is real, right here and now, completely,
and how about if
    you're just a little kid, fast asleep,
    dreaming of the starship *Enterprise*
    gliding deeper into deepest space
    toward who knows what unimaginable adventures
    and illuminated moments of being—
    so fast asleep not even a Klingon laser strike
        could wake you—
and she smiles and whispers,
    "You and me, sweetheart—
how about it?"

Necessary Angels

1952

When I was seven years old
I whispered into my belt buckle,
A secret radio:
"Dragon 4 Starcruiser calling Base,
Dragon 4 Starcruiser calling Base . . ."
And I remember that splurge of joy
When a voice on the other end
Responded rich and clear,
"Come in, Captain Jimmy, come in . . ."

1990

"Return to Base, Captain Jimmy.
Do you read me?
You're about to leave the screen.
Come back, Captain Jimmy!
Return to Base!
Oh, Captain Jimmy,
You dumb shit."

Prayer Bones

Bone is just a sound you make in your throat,
a shaped breath, a word,
till you touch
the smooth massive skull of a feral boar
or balance a pelican's
almost weightless wing bone
across the palm of your hand.

The blood and roots
that bind us to a place
remain sheer romance,
a grand abstraction,
till you slip the quivering heart from a deer
and fry it for breakfast.
Till you pick chanterelles,
or munch baby carrots
as you thin the rows.
We kill to nourish ourselves
on the light released in death,
for we only know what enters us
through these diaphanous membranes
we call our bodies, these whirls
of wind, rain, mineral, and light.

My mind was an idea about itself
till I found the skull of our mule, Red,
beside a fern-shrouded spring
deep in a tan oak thicket
where he had fallen or laid down to die
almost two years earlier.
The constant rush of spring water
has stripped his skull to a dazzling white,
startling among all that green,

the clear water swirling in the brain cavity,
pouring through the sinuses and eye sockets.

After a meandering sluice down the long ravine
the spring water joins the Wheatfield Fork of the Gualala,
then the main stem at the end of the ridge,
and finally slides into the Pacific.

May it take millennia of rain to wear away our bones,
centuries of slow, voluptuous letting go.

Magic and Beauty

Man was able to exert and sometimes enforce his will upon nature, but he could do nothing to ensure the hunter's success. The capture, it seemed, depended upon something beyond the scope of work or technique, upon some other world whence man was shut out at least while working, while imbued with the notions and rhythms of logical efficacity.
—GEORGES BATAILLE

The cave paintings at Lascaux
are unnecessarily beautiful,
though perhaps magic, to enjoin,
makes beauty a necessity.

But since magic resides in the act itself,
in the expropriation of the moment,
we must imagine the hunters rising at dawn
and walking into the earth.

Each carries, in a stone vessel,
a single color, gift of the sun,
beaten from root or berry.
Perhaps they've fasted and kept silent

and sat naked under the stars;
and now, their dreams preceding them,
maybe chanting to prepare their hearts,
they walk deep into the cave

and gather in the torch-flickered, glittering gallery
where each, in turn, will be lifted,
risen to appease
the strength and elegance of his prey,

to touch his fear, his hunger, his heart,
to know, as the hand does not hesitate

in the sweep of the bison's horn,
that magic requires nothing,

it's like stone,
and the beauty
called through our bodies
remains in our bones.

Day Moon

FOR MORRIS GRAVES

It's what the minnow
Clasped in the soft beak
Murmurs to the hooded Spirit-Bird
Bearing her from liquid to liquid;

What shoe leather chants to the road;
Sleepers whisper to their dreams;
What seaweed sighs to waves,
Seed to wind, word to breath;

It's what the boar, scooped by Vishnu
From the end of every exhalation
Like a coal to rekindle this garden of fevers,
Says with such tender and weary marvel:

"Each time
        you carry me
                this way."

Karma Bird

Invisible and shrill,
the Karma Bird rides on your shoulder
like some gruesome offspring
of Long John Silver's crusty parrot
and the raven that haunted Poe's brain.
It's clamped on your shoulder to remind you
that what's purchased at the spirit's expense
invariably falls due,
that what you give is finally what you get,
and what you get is yours.

So when karma curves 'round,
as it assuredly does,
that crass, gleeful bird goes crazy,
hopping up and down on your clavicle
while screeching righteously in your ear,
"Kar-ma! Kar-ma! Kar-ma!"
till you want to strangle the little fucker,

anything to shut him up.
For though it's true
we act in constant ignorance
and often fail the faith we try to keep,
we're wise to accept
all consequences as deserved–
but that doesn't mean you have to like it,
much less love that demented bird.

The Tunnel

AN ELEGY FOR JACK SPICER

The poem ends when the feeling's gone.
When the little boats enter
the Tunnel of Love
empty, driven
by some vast clanking machinery
like the heart.
Like the darkness that comes for your bones
when you're lost
in the tunnel alone.

Carnivals. Poems. Whiskey and blood.
The little girl who wanted to dance at all the parties.
The little boy who slept on her grave.
Dreaming them
as the garbage truck grinds up Cummings Road,
rumbling toward the dump
with a load of spoiled honey,
with lemons and seagulls and funhouse mirrors,
old love letters and busted luck.

Dreaming the boy and girl holding hands
as their little boat enters
the tunnel where language is not enough to save you.
Trying to hold on to their hands
and the darkness and the tunnel and the feeling.
Alice-in-Wonderland hacked to pieces
and buried under the parking lot.
The first lunatic ghoul of a phoneme
screaming in the black tunnel.

Trying to balance
the elegant bone-crystal power of the simple

and the howl clawing your lungs.
Between heartbeat and silence and another
	ragged heartbeat
holding on to the torn ticket for dear life.
Waiting all night for the word that meant
little girl dancing, that led the readers
among wizards and demons, helped them
fashion their own faces from the mud.

The poem ends when the feeling's gone.
When the ruined body collapses in the elevator,
beaten by poems and darkness,
by lovers and whiskey and mirrors,
by the playful glittering nonsense
and the infinitely small vocabulary of our feelings.
The tunnel where words mean nothing. No thing. None.
Not the boy or girl or the bones of their hands
	picked clean.

Unable to speak the feelings that bear them,
breath-to-breath the poem goes on,
into the carnival romance, the danger and blood,
the black tunnel,
the Tunnel of Love,
the tunnels we dig toward each other
in the darkness holding hands.

That's the faith exacted
to endure the famined Sabbath of night,
to wait for the word,
sing for it, cry for it,
beg and curse,
persisting even as we're slaughtered,
even as we fall.

Hagerty Wrecks Another Company Truck

She was stunning, take-me-now-Lord beautiful as she slid out the new Mercedes SL roadster at Eddie Smith's Arco across the intersection, sheen of nylon, endless legs, smiling directly at Bill Hagerty in the Roseburg Timber Company pickup, her hair like honey spilled on the heat, smiling directly and with complete congruent understanding at the blood swelling Hagerty's veins, his nostrils flaring at some phantom fragrance wafting across the baked expanse of asphalt between them, their eyes meeting with a flash of clear purpose. And thus seized, Bill Hagerty smashed into the rear end of an '89 Trans-Am stopped at the light in front of him, glanced off as he wrenched the wheel, hit the curb, nosed up, and impaled the company Ford on a fire hydrant.

Flushed through the sprung door on the geyser of water erupting through the floorboards, Hagerty dislocated his shoulder, cracked two ribs, fractured the pinkie finger on his right hand, and the EMTs were concerned about brain damage as they lifted him into the ambulance, for he kept reaching out with his good arm, moaning, trying to hold the trashed possibilities, the raw promise of that glorious woman in the new Mercedes, now purring into the distance.

Obsession

The flower in the shark's brain
has been perfect for a million years.
The dragon-bloom blood poppy,
carnal and brief,
tattooed at the base of her spine.
The poppy I cut when the petals fall away
to gather the milky lotus of her tears.
Cut in the heat of the day,
blade spiraled around bulb,
fragrant milk
drying black in the sun.
In my mind. In my need
to possess the dense flowering
in my dreams at her breast.
As the shark hits the swimmer,
shaking him apart in its jaws.
Dreams of power and the perfect release
from pain. The bright
flower of it. Blood
blooming in the water,
swirling in her green eyes
like flame.
The hypnotic petal and silk
of her body moving with mine,
the arc of pleasure between dreams
as the poppy blossoms inside me
with the viciously exquisite clarity of obsession.
Diamond condensed a dimension.
Blood expanding as it freezes.

Love Find

After the Oklahoma City bombing,
search-and-rescue dogs
were flown in with their handlers
from all over the U.S.

But when the dogs couldn't find
any survivors
they became disconsolate,

and after another day of nothing
but dead bodies,
if they'd even search
it was desultory at best.

So the handlers began taking turns
hiding in the rubble,
letting the dogs find them alive.

Flux

Driven by the wild equilibrium
at the dynamo core of every thermal exchange,
the cool coastal air,
drawn off the Pacific by the rising Valley heat,
flows inland over the ridge,

and the wind comes up.

Down in the garden
the stalk of a sunflower quivers,
bowed seed head
ready to spill.

Thanks for the Dance

I applaud the way you Pony.
Dig the way you Twist.
Tremble when you hum along
"Do you like it like this?"

I adore the way you Shimmy,
The way you say "Yeah,"
But I live to watch you
Rumba in your underwear.

The Stone

Of two great masters,
They say one died serenely,
A little smile on his face;
The other screaming his head off,
Terrified of death.
There are no conclusions to reach.
The stone falls
Till it hits the earth.

Woman in a Room Full of Rubber Numbers

A woman sits in a straight-backed chair
in a room full of rubber numbers
that move like molecules
near absolute zero. Slower
than slow motion they hit
the square room's walls
and rebound randomly away
to hit another wall, the ceiling, floor, or her,
and away rebound randomly
again. Endlessly.

It doesn't hurt.
The numbers, zero to nine,
the size of doughnuts,
are made of foam rubber
and move so slowly
they're easy to evade.
The woman sits in the chair in the center of the room
and lets them hit her.
She has settled in long past tears,
begging, laughter, or prayer,
a condition she has absorbed
into a powerful resignation
beyond any possibility we might imagine.
She sits there.

No visible exit.
No discernible keeper.
No name.

Reason to Live

I was 22 years old the summer of '67, house-sitting
my brother's place on G Street in Arcata, caught up
seriously for the first time in the flush and struggle of
writing poetry, so poor I couldn't afford a dirt sandwich.
But that day the landlord had hired my idle hands to
help him unload a U-Haul full of his recently deceased
aunt's belongings, paid me ten bucks, and I was crossing
G Street to the Safeway where Wildberries is now,
money hot in hand—enough, tightly rationed, for a week
of spaghetti—and I remember I was laughing that a week
of pasta sure beat my buddy Funt's infamous Starving
Poet Tacos (a slice of bologna on a cold tortilla, roll it
up and munch), laughing and snapping the ten-spot,
goofing on Funt, just crossing the parking lot when I
found Julie, naked in the forest, singing in a language I'd
never heard—Julie with the twisted cross she'd tattooed
between her navel and auburn pubic hair with a dull
safety pin and India ink in a curtained bath at the Girls
Reformatory: it had taken her two hours but the nuns,
she said, wouldn't stop her because they were afraid to
see her naked, and to tell the truth, so was I, but I didn't
let fear stop me, and I'm glad, because 30 years later my
lips still burn where I kissed that cross after we shared
the spaghetti I made, and I'll remember that night for-
ever as the time I figured out that money and food and
poetry were ways to live, not reasons.

Scratch

Whipping a stolen '81 T-Bird convertible across the desert
   on a star-flung summer night,
      top down, tunes cranked up to blast–
       Stones, Dylan, Van the Man–
a half-pound of trainwreck weed on the seat
    between you and a laughing strawberry blond
      with legs from here to Heaven
        who you picked up hitching out of Barstow
   leaving a dipshit husband behind
     along with a lot of a young girl's dreams–
      though she understands
        there's an innocence we never lose,
          and if you're going her way,
she's always wanted
   to walk out on a third-story balcony naked
    in the French Quarter during Mardi Gras
      just to feel the night on her body–
and sure, none of this is even close to love,
   but sometimes you've just got to scratch to get by.

Salvage

Love is the salvage of rapture.
A house built with lumber taken up
from the fallen-down dance hall
abandoned along Austin Creek
when Cazadero was a resort town.

Salvaged, stacked, hauled away;
the old square nails pulled,
new ones driven.
Patient, passionate, plumb, and true.

A house began at the end of a wrecking bar
and finished with shingles lapped in courses,
hammered down tight
against the hell-bent February winds
and the rainy-day raptures of flight.

A house big enough for privacy,
solid enough to hold the light,
the roof caulked at every seam
and the floor of maple tongue-and-groove
already worn smooth

by a thousand midnight waltzes
when it was Spring and the moon was full
and dancers seemed to glide on air,
the men nervously handsome,
the women with flowers in their hair.

Ghost town salvage, built from scratch.
Built by faith, and sweat, and care.
Listening into the materials hard enough to hear

the dancers' laughter drift downstream
and puzzle the otters and owls.

Built of the pleasures that last beyond relief.
Built by the exacting of the real.
The refinement, not the seizure.
The diamond cutter,
not the diamond thief.

Plumb, square, and true.
The house way out at the end of the ridge.
The diamond in the dancers' minds.
The amazing emptiness of moonlight
flooding the dance floor.

An Epithalamium for Victoria

ON THE OCCASION OF OUR MARRIAGE, OCTOBER 7, 1994

I touch your cheek
and another teleologist dies
of an apparent heart attack in a Fresno motel,
the ninth this week,
and the coroner is noticing similarities:
all men over 40;
first names beginning with the letter *D*;
all found clad only in pale blue boxer shorts
    from Mervyn's,
size Medium;
all displaying the same questionable use
    of the semi-colon
in the anguished poems about their childhoods
left uncompleted on the chipped Formica desktops.
And that just when I touch your cheek.

When I touch your throat
(O sweet swooning Jesus and the radiantly
    melting Buddha, too)
every tweed-weenie professor
who has mistaken an impenetrable vocabulary
    for knowledge
and every high school teacher who has lied to a class
is struck dumb at the toll of midnight;
and all the politicians in the Western Hemisphere
drop to their knees, begging forgiveness;
and the last practicing existentialist,
after years of contemplating the intrinsic being
    of an apple,
finally eats it.

Which moves me to kiss you

(Ah, lunar delirium; oh, raw unending diamond nova
    of the sun)
and when our lips touch
every bird in flight folds its wings and glides,
and every bird at roost and babe unborn
dreams of turning its belly to the sun,
and the Northcoast is lashed with two weeks of
    torrential rain
until a man snaps, screams
"There ain't no head like steelhead,"
and hurls himself from the Hiouchi Bridge
    into the swollen Smith
while an old woman in buckskins and cowboy boots
drops osprey feathers on the spot he hit, chanting
"Take him home, Momma, take him home."

Meanwhile, as our kiss continues
on the balcony of the Museum of the Future,
I feel honey swirl in my loins
(oh, thick golden nurture! ah, happy bees!)
and every tree for 500 miles deepens its green,
cones open, pods split and spill,
plum saplings bow to the rising storm
and a majestic old sugar pine rocks on its roots—
and then the balcony tears loose
and we're falling, still in each other's arms, falling . . .

And no, it hasn't all been a romp through the buttercups,
but after 30 years more or less shared,
of catch-as-catch-can, itch and scratch,
four-lane all-night fliers that left us dirty side up
    in the ditch,
of handing our asses to the gods above
while digging our toes in the earth,
I'd say we're still falling,
falling in love.

Falling into Place

It astounds and delights me
on a planet with a 24,000-mile circumference
and a surface area of 96,000,000 square miles
to be here
at 2,000 feet in the Klamath Mountains
on the long wild ridge separating
the Middle and South Forks of the Smith
in a tight, dry cabin
on a freezing, moonless November night
snuggled down on the couch
by the wood heater
with my sweetheart
and our child.

Play-By-Play

Playing Wiffle ball near dusk
with Jason, just turned six,
soft summer evening
deep in the hills,
I serve to pitch and announce:
"Here it is, a three-one fastball
to young Jason Dodge,
and—on my god—he turns on it,
deep drive, dead center,
way back, absolutely *crushed*,
a white speck vanishing over the garden fence,
long gone
like a turkey through the corn—
so far outa here
they'll have to send out a search party."

And folks, that's the thrill
of turning one around,
of getting it *all*,
dead mortal solid on the sweet spot,
riding the bolt
of power into flight.

Jason, so pleased
he's about to burst out of himself,
says, "Go get the ball.
There's still plenty of light."

Job Application

I want to lie on an open hillside
and feel everything
quicken in the light.
I don't want to think, judge, decide.
It's been a tough winter.
Vicky's father died in November.
A month later, I found
my brother dead
in his Klamath cabin.
Then a month of rain,
flooding, slides.
Down in the frost-seared garden,
ravens perched on the scarecrow.

I want to flop down on a grassy hillside
and let it all rise on the heat.
Give myself utterly to the flourishing.
Bury my face in the massed poppies;
turn my face to the sky.
If I must work, may the task
match my flagging power
and meet my true ambition:
to feel the roots dig deeper
while I imagine
new colors for a flower.

The Mouth of the River

Closing her eyes to intensify the sensation
she touches a warm stone to her cheek.
He's moved so completely
a man of less experience might have swooned—
while he, nearing 50 years, merely staggers,
his moan choked to a whimper,
puddled with desire,

yet lucid enough to appreciate
his utter confusion about what he feels
for this young woman,
and what, if anything, he should do.
Motives are seldom pure,
but he's not even sure
what he wants to be:

the stone, its warmth, her cheek,
the river, ocean, or the sun inside
the moon burning inside her—
all, none, or some complex combination of possibilities
that he knows enough to know eludes him.
But he knows beyond knowledge
that the rain-swollen river, strong and slow,

moves the way she would be touched,
and he wants to open his hands and touch her like that,
at the melting threshold between glide and swept,
swirling borders, rolling depths,
Mozart weaving milky emerald silk,
all caught and curled in that flowing poise
of wet coil, chrome spark.

The Prior and Subsequent Heavens

In the night's most present moment—
non-duplicable, gone—
the starlight on our faces
was a million light-years old.
I changed.
You changed too.
The light went on.

We change beyond choice,
bound to the universe
as congruent events
of its endless origin
as well as its momentary whereabouts,
each breath and heartbeat subject
to an absolute relative
spatio-temporal plenitude
of possibilities, delusions, and births,
arrangements and derangements,
properties, principles, and mysterious powers,
some as strict as gravitation,
some as random as a lizard in the soup.

You change it.
I do too.
I was trying to write the history of an instant,
to sustain the exact point
where it opened into song,
joined the sunlight shaping the river,
the starlight on our faces,
the fire under the bubbling soup.
You dove from the opposite shore
and swam toward me with the moon in your throat,
body gliding underwater

like the shadow of a bird.
Your passage changed the current,
changed the river,
changing you and me.

What we know is never the same.
It scatters like starlight in the mind;
fades into the future it creates:
nothing lost, nothing gained, going on
as the mutable condition of mortal grace.

This starlit song began along the river,
singing with you in the summertime dusk,
barefoot and cuddled on the cooling sand
waiting for the stars to emerge in this world,
as the slow green river gathered our shadows,
singing at the top of our voices
till our toes curled,
and I changed into you changing too.
Not for ever, maybe,
but for sure.

Old Growth

They wheel my gurney into the colonoscopy
    procedure room,
a procedure for which I've been prepped by a night
of GI lavage, employing an inaptly named laxative
    called "Go-Lightly,"
followed by two tap-water enemas,
cleansing my alimentary canal so thoroughly
I imagine my intestines as shiny as chrome at a
    roadster show–
shiny, that is, except for the blood that has brought
    me here,
having lost half my red-cell volume by the time
I wobbled into the ER, entering the trajectory
that has landed me behind the closing doors of
    Colonoscopy Central
and forced the realization that my body is wearing out,
and an appreciation for a homily that hits it right
    on the screws:
                Old age isn't for weaklings.
I know that I, who have spent some heart and
    spirit fighting
those who use their power to keep others powerless,
now must fight this failing body that carried me,
not without stagger and swagger,
through sex, drugs, and rock 'n' roll,
that remained fast to its findings when the
    bullhorns crackled,
                    "Disperse now or be arrested,"
that buckled numbly at the riot sticks' blows,
yet swirled into water at a sweetheart's touch,
a body that has borne the sally of my going forth
into this grandly mad adventure called "consciousness,"
tenor as much as vehicle, body of its own metaphor,

a 3-D tripod for the psyche's movie camera,
and after reckless decades of excess and neglect–
running lucky, running fast–
Time, without regret, has called its markers due,
and I find my life thus far has suddenly come to this:
they're about to slip a miniature camera up my ass,
an event certainly preferable to death,
but the first deep indignity accompanying
     inescapable decay,
and it's the first time since I was a little kid I've felt
     so helpless.
Yet almost immediately I'm helped by the anesthesiologist
who pumps a potent mix of Demerol and Versed,
narcotic braided with the hypnotic, through my IV
     into me, myself, and I, aye,
aye, I'm dissolving,
the lake freezing from the top down,
and for no discernible reason that defiant
     five-year-old kid inside me
digs into that wild dignity at the core of rage,
and I understand, with unshakable delight,
that my will to fight is stronger than my feebling flesh,
and at that point of eclipse I have a vision:
I and thousands like me, hordes of psychedelic relics,
pie-eyed dreamers, pantheists with Taoist proclivities,
Trotskyite bandits from the emerald hills,
all standing together,
wrinkled, twisted, worn, tweaked,
aging and infirm yet somehow indomitable,
fighting hard for what we love and what remains:
family, friends, freedom, justice, and ancient forests.
So heed fair warning, corporate heads and greedy
     running-dogs,
mergered oligarchs swathed in the baffle of bureaucrats
     and bought politicians,
you mess with us at the risk of grief:

not to mention our dentures latched on your fat asses
   like deranged snapping turtles;
the Corridors of Power rendered treacherously slippery
   with our long drool-strings of Malt-o'-Meal;
we'll hack into your laptops the old-fashioned way,
   with canes, crutches, walkers, axes, splitting mauls,
   anything handy;
the Emphysema Brigade, left breathless by decades of
   Lucky Strikes and trainwreck weed,
will beat you senseless with oxygen bottles;
every time you present another lying THP from
   your pimp scientists
we'll drown you out with cranky shouts of
   "Huh? What?";
you get in our dish, you better defend all your
   self-righteous bullshit or we'll slap you upside
   the head with our soaked Depends
or strangle you with our catheters, or with a rope
   braided of the weird hairs
now growing from strange places on our bodies—
   ears, eyebrows, elbows, nipples—
and if that doesn't work, we'll tie you spread-eagled on
   that desk of yours bigger than most of our kitchens
and beat on you with our colostomy bags
(and if we don't have half the energy we did
   in our youth,
refinement, I assure you, has tripled the efficiency
   of its application
in whipping ass on soul-killing systems);
and if nothing else works we'll call a General Strike
and then stage a massive occupation of your
   headquarters' suites
where we'll make you listen to our every bodily woe,
how our hearts and livers are wearing out
and our patience already worn thin—

yes we'll force you to listen to endless shifts of us
    old farts
describe in interminable detail our rising bile levels,
    EKGs, EEGs, CAT scans,
blood panels, liver function, ingrown toenails,
    and every bowel movement for the last two weeks,
and generally bore you into madness unless you
    change your ways.

Three Ways to Get the Carrot on the Stick

A sudden magnificent leap.
Eliminate hunger.
Break the stick.

Eurydice Ascending

She'd always been a sucker for musicians.
And Orpheus was magnificent:
his songs had enchanted
both birds and arrows from the sky.
But like all of them
he was a child.
The eager need, the boyish charm,
the endless innocence of his singing.
He moved her, yes,
he was sweet, playful, attentive, there;
but he didn't take her away.
Hades was different.
He didn't confuse
his power with the power
of her surrender.
He held nothing back,
not even his fear,
and everything that wasn't answered
in the one flesh of their body
was obliterated.

When Orpheus came down for her,
silencing the underworld
with his desolate song,
Hades listened, and was moved.
He had no honorable choice
except to permit her return,
but he wisely made provision:
Orpheus couldn't look back.

She knew he would.
He was a poet, probably
already writing his triumph in his head.

She knew he would
if he heard her weeping,
and as she followed him up toward the light of the world
she began crying softly.
Orpheus stopped,
his hair crowned in the honeyed light spilling from above,
and for a long time stared straight ahead
before he turned.
It was the first time she could remember
he didn't say anything. Not a word.
Just nodded, looking sad,
a flicker of pout,
then, as she faded, turned
and continued his journey,
or whatever that dream-babble song was
he believed was his journey.

The Drought of '76

Lungworm and pig shit,
heat-shimmered tin,
steel ringing on steel,
musk of deer flesh,
sweet rot of apples,
peeled paint, peeled skin,
sweat stinging blisters,
hole in the crankcase,
tarweed, ammonia, oil cloth, lye,
piss running on dust before it soaks in.

True Account of the Saucer People

I was just hoeing up some peas
when this flying saucer landed
and these forces got out
(I call 'em forces 'cause you can't see 'em
but you can feel 'em there with you—
heck, that's real hard to explain)
anyway, they started talking, not in our words
but understood in the English lingo
right away in your own head
(geez, that's even harder to explain)
and one was cussing the other out
I don't remember exactly
but something like, "You dummy,
you always land on some cracker-ass farmer—
now go get the relativizer
and blast him down to safe time,"
and this other force yarded out a contraption
that you *could* see, looked like
a blue metal circle inside a silver metal circle,
only all throbbing and a-humming,
and this contraption took a dead bead on me
and 'fore I could even think to run or duck
damn if straight off I got feeling
tireder than a plowing mule at sundown,
and though I started right out
it's took me two weeks just to get here to tell you
and I 'spect they're gone by now.

About Time

1

Oh, the jewel in the lotus, ahhhh.
Right now.
Joy in the heart of the moment.
Right now.
The heat of the moment.
This instant.
Blossom of the moment.
Time is a sphere
and the moment right now
the still center
through which everything flows,
a raft meandering with the river,
an easy ride for angels of the Tao.
Always now.
Before you were born,
after you die:
now.

2

Time runs through angels
like rivers through canyons.
Of course, angels may only be
the space between the river
and the canyon rim,
the emptiness left
after water erodes
what was there
away.

3

My brother Bob
was no angel.

Bob's dead now
but I remember him
like a river in a canyon,
and probably because of the constant pain
he lived with from a ruined leg,
he took refuge when he could
in the blossom of the moment.
I remember one night,
having finished
his seventh spliff of killer,
he nodded and announced,
"Screw the past.
It already happened."

Rivers don't run backward.
You remember the river maybe
where you crossed it,
or where you stopped for lunch
at the falls in late spring,
but you remember it now,
the blossom of the moment,
and if I have tears on my cheeks
because Bob isn't here
to remember it with me—
the flash of the kingfisher,
the banded cream and ash
of alders shivering in the downstream breeze—
time doesn't stop—
the river slides through the canyon,
pools, falls;
and Bob was right
the past is over,
done, gone,
but I'm not sure,
a sob caught in my throat,
whether I'm the one

waving good-bye
from the bank
or the boat.

4

There's a story,
probably apocryphal,
that when the Taoist master Lao-tzu
was passing into the wilderness
one of the guards at the frontier
recognized him and pleaded,
"Oh Master, leave us your wisdom
on the mystery of time,"
to which Lao-tzu, riding his donkey,
turned and laughed over his shoulder,
"Too late to stop now."

4A

In another version of the story
Lao-tzu turns his donkey around
and rides back to the guard,
reaches down and touches his shoulder,
looks into his eyes, and says,
"I can tell you this for sure:
The future is always on time
and your ass better be there."

5

The duration of a moment
is best measured
as the length and depth of time
required to say:
"Meet me in the French Quarter at midnight."
(Though I personally favor
"You must go now.")

6

It may be that not all nows
are of equal duration
(the hydraulic position)
or that they are
(the mechanistic view)
or that they are
experienced differently
by different people
(the experiential notion).
A huge argument about this,
the nature of time, rages,
and some of the boys have begun
calling each other dreadful names
like "dithering shithead," "moron," and "angel."
Now, now.

7

"Time,"
Rexroth wrote,
"is the mercy of eternity."
Which doesn't mean for a minute
that you can expect
mercy from time.
Gregory Peck
shot in the back.
The patchy cream and ash
of alder bark.
Your hand in mine,
both of us looking
up at the big screen
and crying,
O nameless sorrow,
and a meanness
in the world–

sometimes
just too damn much.
The stranger in the same aisle,
who arrived in the purple
'56 Ford,
calls over, "Don't feel bad.
You know, the great thing about life
is you get till you die
to decide if it's worth it.
That's plenty of time."
The man sitting behind us
says under his breath,
"Shit,
they shot
Gregory Peck
in the back.
What's *that*
all about?"
And on-screen
the bandito who shot him
kicks Gregory Peck in the ribs,
hard,
to make sure
he's dead,
then pushes back his sombrero
and eases the hammer down on his stolen Colt.
He says to Gregory Peck's body
lying in the blood-soaked dust,
"It's about time,
amigo."

Moments ago now.

And just then,
that long, slow,
forlorn cry.

And when we finished weeping
we walked out of the movie about time,
still holding hands,
into the late winter afternoon
under a low, scuffed-nickel sky.

Smithereens

Tear this jagged chunk of obsidian from between my
lungs and smash it. Crush it.
Grind it to brilliant dust

and then shovel it back into the diamond nova,
feed it to the furnace of roots,
to the million-year-old flower

perfect in the shark's brain,
the tiny crimson poppy tattooed at the base of her spine,
then walk down to the river and open your hands

so I can touch you through the bars of the rain,
feel the obliterating clarity of skin,
feel whatever we can imagine together,

feel it till we finally understand
that when we die, the soul
leaves the body through the fingertips.

Jack o' Hearts Shopping Mortmart

Mechotek music on the jukebox, Jack–
no savvy da lingo dere,

not down with the chops.
Caught in the corrosive scour of narcosis,

candled in the oxycodone light,
dropping them by the fistful, by the tub,

pain killer pills to keep you bearably numb,
because for the last decade you've been running

through the tunnels between dreams,
brain burning like dry pitch,

banging on every closed stone door
with your tin cup

so long now you
can't remember what dreams are for

or when hope blinked to blank.
What goes down, is down, stays down.

Fear of the dark.
Of the whip, the grid, the rockets;

the robot milking your loins
for the last sweet drop.

Holy Shit

PART ONE: THE MANTLE OF CHAOS
Light is information without a message.
        –MARSHALL MCLUHAN

1

We fueled up and finally got going so fast
we were jacking gas straight to the modems,
slamming electro dino-juice smack into our cerebellums
through a hot-wire skull hole
laser-tapped so the 'plug could be
torqued right down to the bone–
that way the internal combustion couldn't blow
our bubbling brain jelly
all over the map of ashes
whose fine print (which nobody ever read)
said *Stop*!
        Too late.
                We couldn't.

Mile after mile
the ravaged fields fly by.

Now we know so much
that knowledge has overwhelmed knowing,
and discoveries come far too fast for reflection.

2

Too many dots in the logic-model
where making the dots be God was sort of the point
and connecting them
the generative force
for more dots you might want to make,
maybe to market as wild horses
mating in the timberline rain.

Blown out, sold out, worn out—
as if the electromagnetic field suddenly flickered, flipped,
or folded ass-side up
plumb into the vagrant slippage, slop,
and randomly relative pressure drops
which mark the shifting center of chaos—
for us, less a quantum flop
than a wanton leap that didn't quite reach
even the edge of an Eden
almost reconstructed
from the original pieces
despite throwing away the instructions with the box.

We are left where we find ourselves:
maze-burned rats trapped in our carbon cages,
spinning in hyperdimensional domains
like biobotic protein strings
chained to the very dots we made
and every dot we find.
And yet we have amazingly remained
within hooting distance of the divine,
despite the spineless cynicism
and the mutilating irony of the age.

3

He turned fifty on a half-moon in early March,
and after a dreamless decade
—empty, inaccessible, or simply not memorable—
he dreamed, that birthday night, of the pocket
          monster Charizard.
Loaded with fire, the 'Zard's pyromaniacal spin
inflicted so many serious hit-points
on multinational capitalism
that a few recent mergers actually unraveled.
So it was a good dream for him, good
in a shamelessly untrammeled way—

pent-up rage released in flaming destruction
certainly has its primal charms–

but dude, you know, it's like *fantasy*,
fly-by-night travel into the High Lonesome
and other destinations
lamentably not real:
you kill the pain with pills
and try to believe one day you'll join
that mythic, merry band
of Trotskyite bandits roaming the hills,
relieving the rich of undistributed surplus
and passing it on to the poor.
Heck, at his age it's an act of faith
to even seek a state of grace
in this bloated cultural commodity spectacle
of locked doors and cheap thrills.
Spicer, you lit the lamp:
at the center of creation
cries a longing for oblivion.

So who can blame you
if you finally give in
and dream up a shaman kneeling
with an obsidian blade
to cut the throat of a psalmist.
The psalmist begs, "No. Please. I'm a Lutheran."
The shaman smiles kindly and slices the carotid,
        explaining,
in that oblique Zen way he's copped from watching
        martial arts movies,
"Yeah, and I'm a marsupial."
Dig his inscrutably cool, deconstructed chops,
but blood is blood, whatever the style points,
and the blood mixes with benzene in the burning river,
smoke curls around the plutonium doorknobs

and momentarily blinds the ten-pound rats
feeding in the landfill nursery.
To escape the whole mutating mess—dreamed up,
     remember?—
the shaman, riding salmon-bellied clouds,
floats away at sunset until he finally settles
high in a big-leaf maple deep in the wilderness.
For a hundred years the shaman gathers blood
     through the tree's tangled roots,
draws it from weasels, bears, tanagers, turtles, voles—
from every creature that has died in the sweet
     maple shade—
and then the shaman sends it back,
particle and wave, into the singer's body/breath
so the cracks in Heaven are patched by dawn
and the sleeping children never dream
     how close they came to death.
The shaman dies during the transfusion
(man, my red corpuscles are in mass confusion)
and life, in all its implacable matter-of-factness, goes on.

PART TWO: LIVING IN THE REAL WHIRL

> *The significant problems we face cannot be solved at the same
> level of thinking we were at when we created them.*
>   —ALBERT EINSTEIN

A space for everything and everything
riding the wild swoop and swirl of flux, the hurl and blur
of living in the real whirl.
Check out the old stuttering projector at the
     Rancho Deluxe Drive-in Church:
its unreconstructed light
barely reaches the tattered screens
we bring to see our movies shown
at the little sundance festivals of our selves.
Oh, what a glorious mess of transparency and emulsion,

of confusion that'll screw you into the ground
and a dreamcast light to lift you back up,
all the fracture and fusion,
fucking and fighting,
the seethe of ego, the fury and swill
of self-interest, nightmare, and sweet dreams—
you gotta love it. Especially if you're selling
indulgences at the concession stand.

But knowing the steps to the dance
is not the same as dancing,
where getting lost in the music means
feeling your feet on the earth
and your body part of the landscape
that joins the movie to actual movement
by crossing the Bridge of Dreams
spanning the real roar and swirl of the unnameable river
whose water is everywhere it is writ upon.
Don't matter, Jack, if you don't give a shit
what the dance means
or even if you can hear the music
or see the screen.
You can't escape the light, sound, action:
they're as much a fact as photons or amino acid strings,
as real as wave or stone, wind and wheat.
We live inside the music and the light,
dance even while sitting still,
another shiver spun off the drum skin,
another whirl in the whirling.
So dive right in, understanding
that you live by life,
live inside the wave, inside the light,
and all you truly have to do
is what you believe is right.

PART THREE: HOLY SHIT
The need for mystery is greater than the need for an answer.
—KEN KESEY

I believe in the scarlet archangels
hurled from the star-birth infernos
coalescing in collapsing space:
I believe in their swords of light.
I believe in the windstorm that ripped
the top off the sugar pine snag
and blew it eighty yards out on the pond.

I believe in the four-year-old furiously pedaling
        his tricycle,
the eleven-year-old barrel racer, ponytail flying,
the dust of moments blown through our bodies,
syncopation of blood and breath.
I believe in everything and nothing at once,
the life roaring through us
like water cascading down stone palisades
into a bottomless alpine lake.

I believe the stories
of those who've danced on the roof of oblivion,
those who've smeared their bodies
with ashes and apricot blossoms
and went dreaming among the waves,
those who laugh, who scream, who never speak—
I believe you.

I believe in the power, point, and absolute purpose
of a pod of killer whales ramming
a yearling grey whale
to death in the Chukchi Sea.
I believe in the osprey fledgling crunched in a
        wolverine's jaw,

in the mother's talons slashing its flesh,
in the wolverine's blood twisting down the
        sun-bleached snag,
in egg and empty nest.
I believe the spine-shot deer baa-ing like a lamb;
the shrill, frenzied, mortal shriek of the young raccoon
as the dogs overwhelmed her and tore her to pieces
on the frost-glittered banks of Redwood Creek;
the grey squirrel's eerie, almost electronic chirp–
a sound like a flat rock skittering across a frozen pond–
as I carried his broken body off the road.

I believe the muffled blast of the .410 shotgun
after Billy Reeder held his breath for what seemed forever
and then with an utterly forsaken cry
pulled the trigger and blew his big toe off
so he wouldn't be sent to Vietnam.

I believe in the breath of an old woman dreaming
the wind carries her across the sky.
I believe every huckleberry leaf,
every alder, owl, crane fly, toad,
every steelhead's chrome shimmer upriver,
every catkin and apple,
each song, poem, and breath.

I believe in the confluence of memory and dream,
every wet field, each twirling seed.

I believe a molecule from your brain stem
will be found a thousand years from now
in a woodrat's tiny dry rib-bone
inside an owl pellet
under the Doug fir where you and your sweetheart
will make love while hiking the Lost Coast
a dozen summers from now.

I believe every atom of creation
is indelibly printed with divinity.
I believe in the warm peach
rolled in the palm of my hand.
I believe God plays the saxophone
and the Holy Ghost loves to dance.

And I believe we are born to both fate and chance,
that we're meant to chase ourselves
through the labyrinths of desire,
get lost, slaughtered, and discover
extravagant pleasures lusciously prolonged.
And I believe that you can only attain such detachment
through total, unstinting attachment to this world,
here and now, all, every bit,
by getting your face in it
while throwing your self away.
And I believe we will suffer and suffer and suffer,
and that one joy torches a thousand sorrows,
that today is tomorrow,
that faith is a reflex of gratitude,
and that faith demands we go down singing
rather than dwindle into constant snivel
because existence won't give us what we want.

I believe in every voice in the choir,
every breath-borne note and syllable.
And I believe most of all
my belief is not required.